helpme UNDERSTAND™

Feeling **Insecure** &
Learning ***Confidence***™

AF067452

REAL mvpkids

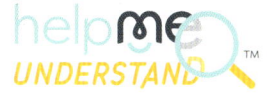

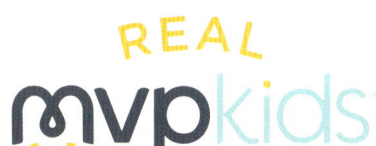

# Sarah Sizes Up the Insecure Ant™

**SOPHIA DAY®**

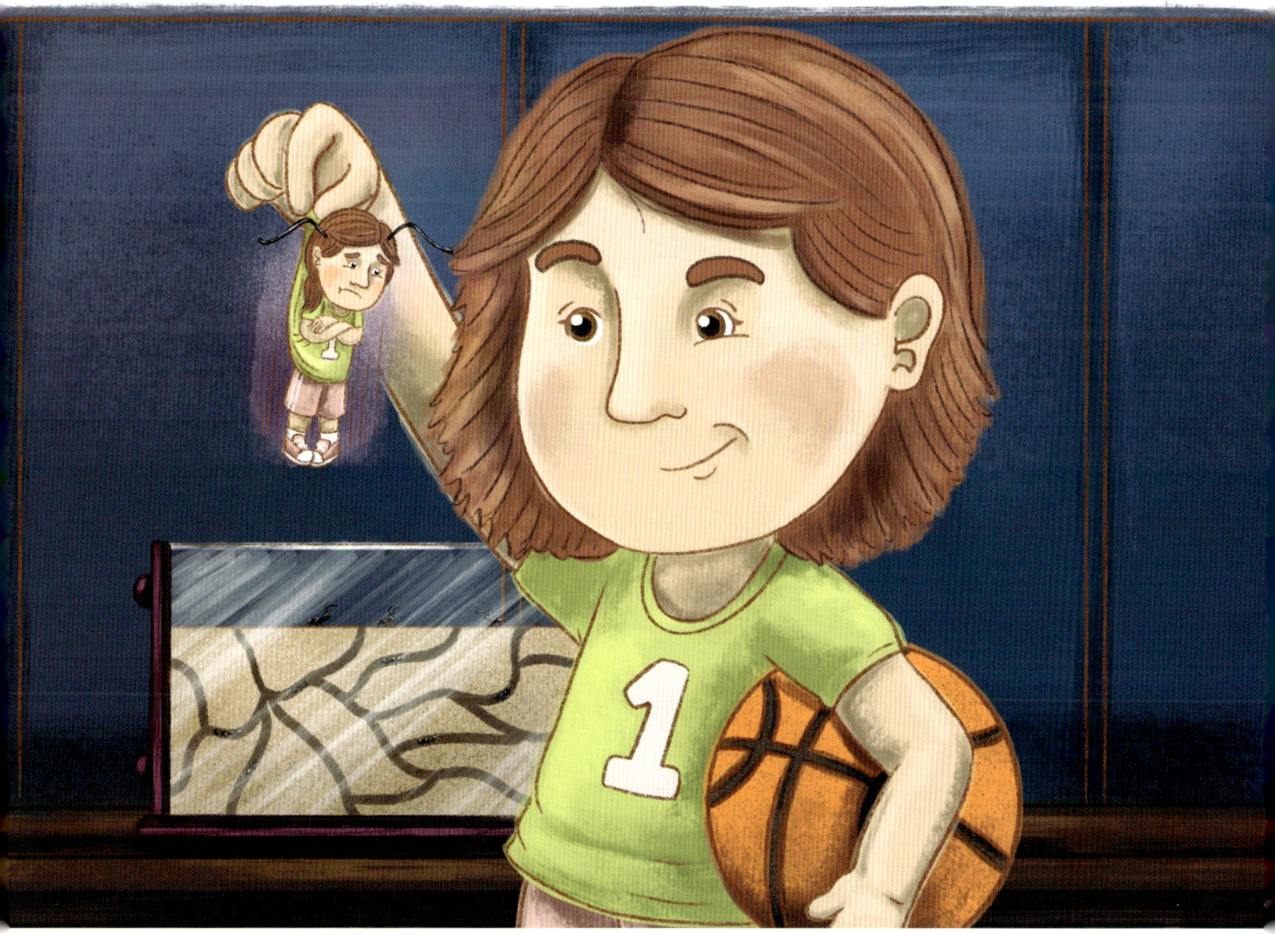

*Written by* Megan Johnson *Illustrated by* Stephanie Strouse

**The Sophia Day® Creative Team-**
Megan Johnson, Stephanie Strouse,
Kayla Pearson, Timothy Zowada,
Celestte Dills, Patty Lopez Gregersen, Mel Sauder

A **special thank you** to our reviewers who graciously give us feedback, edits, and help ensure that our products remain accurate, applicable, and genuinely diverse.

Text and pictures copyrighted © 2020 by MVP Kids Media, LLC

All rights reserved. No part of this publication may be reproduced in whole or in part by any mechanical, photographic, or electronic process, or in the form of any audio or video recording nor may it be stored in a retrieval system or transmitted in any form or by any means now known or hereafter invented or otherwise copied for public or private use without the written permission of MVP Kids Media, LLC.

Published and Distributed by MVP Kids Media, LLC -
Mesa, Arizona, USA
Printed in China

Designed by Stephanie Strouse

DOM Dec 2020, Job # 012-004-01

help me UNDERSTAND™

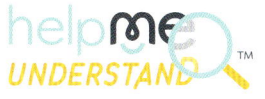

Feeling **Insecure** & Learning ***Confidence***™

REAL mvpkids®

# Sarah Sizes Up the Insecure Ant™

**SOPHIA DAY®**

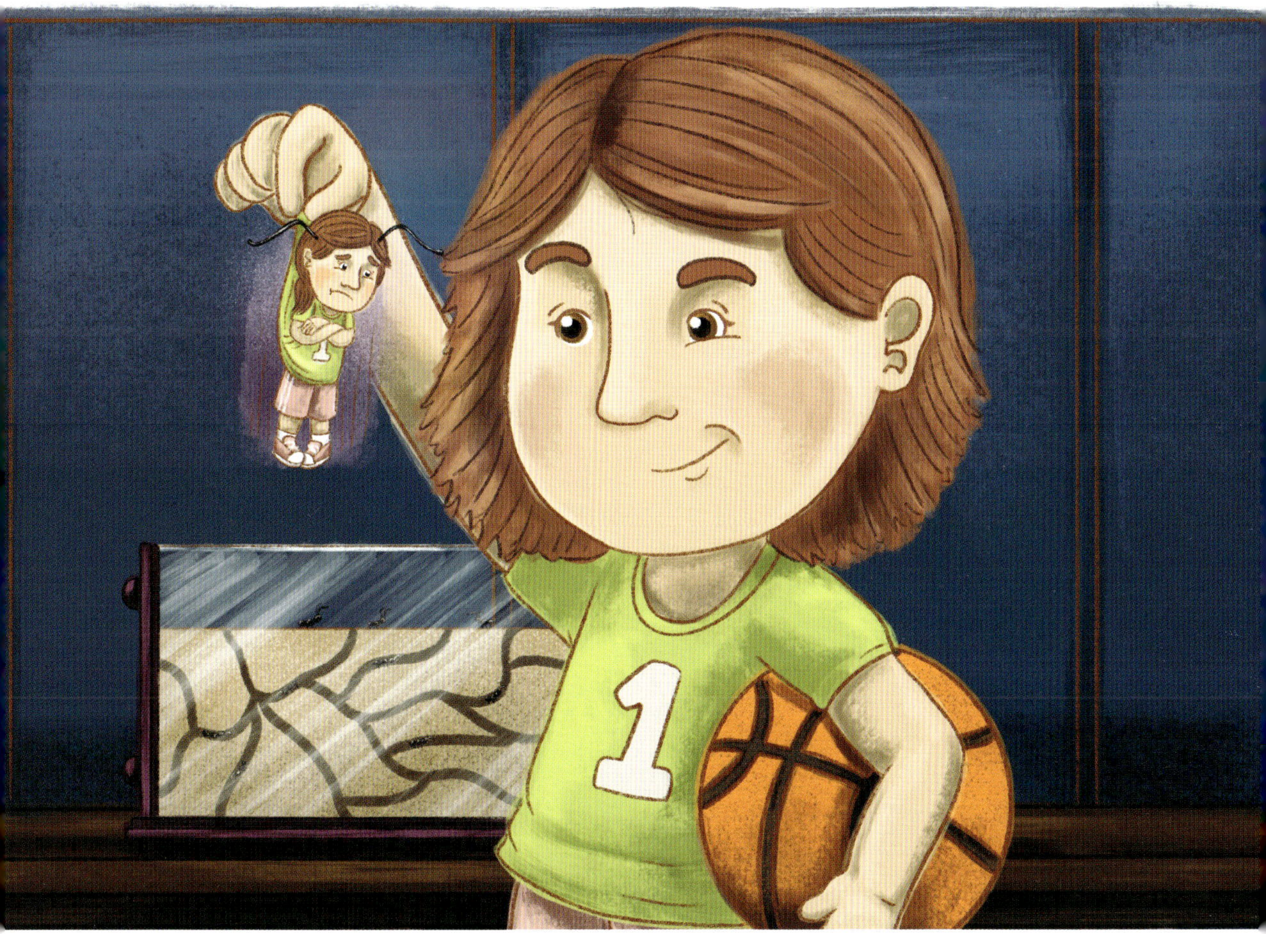


*Written by* Megan Johnson *Illustrated by* Stephanie Strouse

# Sarah never quite felt like she belonged.

She wasn't like other kids. She had different interests, and she was shy. No, she was awkward. Sarah always felt less important, less popular, and less talented than others. She'd give anything just to feel ordinary.

# She was a good student but never raised her hand in class.

Whenever she was called on, her mind would go blank. Just the thought of everyone turning to look at her made her feel sick.

At home, her older brother, David, took the spotlight. Sarah was content to let him have it. She often slipped off to her room unnoticed.

Winter break was coming soon, and Sarah **felt relieved** to have two weeks without all the **awkward moments** at school.

She began daydreaming about building snow forts with Julia ...

... and moving her ant colony into the new deluxe farm she hoped to get for Hanukkah.

But her mom had signed her up for the winter break basketball clinic.

"It'll give you something to do while Dad and I work," she said. "Besides, you might decide to join the team."

Sarah did not want to play on the team.
People would watch the games.
They would watch her.

Just thinking about it made her feel like a tiny ant in a BIG world.

What if she wasn't good at basketball? What if she didn't make any friends? Would she embarrass herself?

When the first day of basketball clinic came, she tried to fight the flutter of dread in her stomach, but she felt

small

and

insecure.

Sarah hesitated at the gym doors. Her sweaty palm slipped down the handle as she pulled the door open.

"Come join our warm-ups," Coach Zavala called.

Sarah surveyed the other players. She saw a group of older kids talking and laughing in the far corner. Sarah's face blushed hot.

Were they laughing *at her*?

"You're all red. Are you okay, Sarah?" Maddie asked. Maddie was the tallest girl in Sarah's grade, and she played basketball every day at recess.

"Um... yeah... I should probably take off my sweatshirt." Sarah was *embarrassed* Maddie could see she was blushing.

*Maybe she would believe she was just hot.*

"Huddle up!" called Coach Zavala.
As all the players came to center court, Sarah sized them up. *Tall, pretty, athletic, popular...* Sarah compared herself to the other kids.

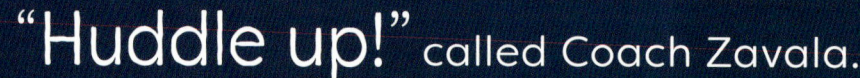

*Little Sarah Ant and the Giants,* she thought to herself.

Sarah was so lost in thought that she missed Coach's directions. Suddenly, everyone was pairing up with a partner, and Sarah began to panic.

She almost **felt relief** when someone tapped on her shoulder, but she turned around ...

... and realized it was Devin. He was a really good player. She was *sure* she'd **embarrass** herself.

Sarah stumbled through the rest of practice in a fog. *I don't belong here,* she thought.

When practice was over, David met her outside to walk home. He high-fived some of the other kids as they passed.

*How does he know EVERYONE?* Sarah wondered.

"How do you DO it?" she asked.

"Do what?" David replied.

"Make friends *so easily*?" Sarah wanted to know.

Then, David gave her some *really* **bad** advice.

"I just pretend they all should know me. I mean, if I'm going to be famous someday, I have to build a fan club, right?" David joked.

"Listen, if you're feeling bad about yourself, start looking for all the flaws in the other kids. You'll figure out you're just as good—or as bad—as they are."

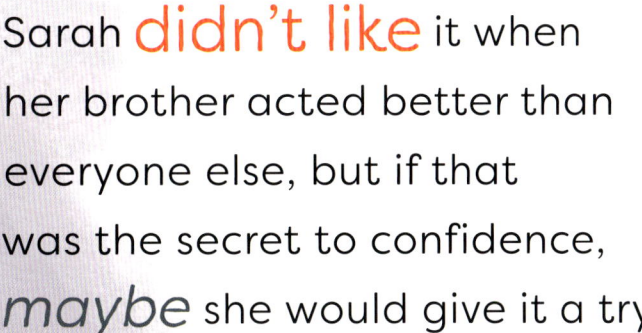

Sarah didn't like it when her brother acted better than everyone else, but if that was the secret to confidence, *maybe* she would give it a try.

The next day, Sarah tried out David's **bad advice.**

*Maddie might be tall,* she thought, *but I'm faster.*

She raced her down the court during warm-ups and gave a triumphant grin.

"*HA!*" blurted Sarah.

Maddie avoided Sarah for the rest of the day.

*I can play tough, too,* Sarah decided.

She blocked Devin, making him lose his balance and fall. For a moment, she felt like the roles were reversed and

# SHE was the GIANT.

But only for a moment.

When Coach called her over to the bench, she felt like she shrank **back down to** ant size.

"See, you don't belong on the team," she said to herself.

Sarah wished she could crawl out of the gym and burrow her way home, where she never had to prove she belonged.

This time, her dad met her outside to walk home. "How was basketball?" he asked.

"I don't know, Dad. I don't really have friends in the camp. I'm not sure I want to play on the team."

Sarah told him about the kids laughing in the corner.

She also talked about her trouble with Maddie and Devin.

"Everyone else is better than me. I spent today trying to see their faults, but it just made me feel worse," Sarah admitted.

"You know, Sarah, comparing yourself with someone else will never make you feel good," said Dad.

# "Do you want to know my secret for confidence?"

"Yes! Tell me, please!" she begged.

"We don't see things the way they are; we see them the way WE are. If you see yourself as a tiny ant, you will be."

"So here are my two keys," he went on. "Improve and encourage."

"I know I need to improve. I'm not—" Sarah began.

"Hold on. Let me explain," her dad interrupted her.

"When you're feeling inferior, remember you're not there to prove yourself; you're there to improve yourself. Be comfortable with who you are instead of wishing you were like someone else. You can shine with the strengths you have."

"Improve, not prove. Got it," confirmed Sarah.

"The next thing is to encourage others. When you're comparing yourself and wondering what others think of you, you're really being self-centered. Instead, focus on others. Try asking a question or giving a genuine compliment."

That night, Sarah's mom helped her write a list of her strengths and how they could help her team. Then, they thought of some encouraging things she could say to the other players.

Mom pretended she was one of the other kids, and Sarah practiced **confidence**—looking others in the eye and standing up straight instead of staring at the floor.

Sarah woke up with a flutter in her stomach. This time, it wasn't dread; it was excitement! Sarah looked in the mirror and said to herself,

"Improve and encourage. I can do this!"

Instead of being distracted by her thoughts, Sarah listened closely to the coach for ways she could *improve* her skills.

When it was time to partner up, she approached Maddie instead of waiting to be chosen.

*"I like your jersey,"* Sarah said.

*"Thanks!"* Maddie smiled widely.

When Devin made a basket, Sarah called out, **"Great shot!"**

"Thanks," said Devin. "Good ball handling." He gave her a high-five and her confidence *soared*.

*Dad was right, Sarah thought. Encouraging others without trying to prove myself really does make me feel more confident.*

After the clinic, Devin asked Sarah if she was going to join the team.

"Yes, I think so," she replied.

"Me too!" said Maddie. "I think we'll make a really good team."

Sarah thought about what makes a good team. "Did you know an ant colony communicates so well that they work like one **big superorganism**\*?!"

*\*A **superorganism** is a highly organized group that functions as one unit.*

*Oops. Oh no.* Thought Sarah. *They'll think I'm silly.*

The dizzy shrinking feeling was coming back.

"WOW! That's *so cool!*" Devin replied. "Maybe you could be our team captain and help us work like that."

Now she could focus on improving her strengths and encouraging others, too!

She didn't feel inferior.

She didn't feel awkward.

She was better than ordinary.

She was confident!

Heart is racing, hands are sweating,
And you want to disappear.
Kids are laughing, and you're guessing
You're the reason that they sneer.

You're shrinking in the background wishing
You could finally find a cure
To the blushing and belittling
When you're feeling insecure.

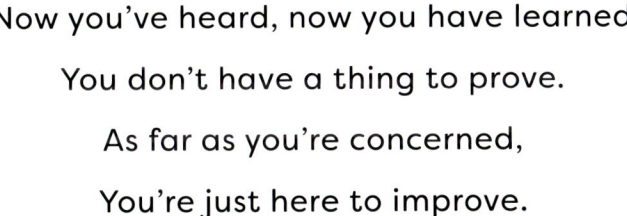

Now you've heard, now you have learned
You don't have a thing to prove.
As far as you're concerned,
You're just here to improve.

You're not perfect, but you do possess
Talents all your own.
Take some time to list your strengths
And all the ways you've grown.

You'll find it's so rewarding
To encourage someone else.
Now your confidence is soaring
With the focus off yourself!

# LEARN & DISCUSS

Feeling insecure or inferior to others gave me a shrinking feeling. I didn't like being the center of attention. My mind would go blank, and I blushed when I was embarrassed. Sometimes I thought people were talking or laughing at me when they really weren't.

*Do you feel like this sometimes?*

*What makes you feel afraid of being yourself around others?*

*Why do you feel like others do not like you?*

Some people seem naturally confident. I asked my brother about how he can be friends with everyone. His advice was to notice the worst in others. I learned quickly that belittling others to boost my own confidence only made me feel worse.

*Think about how you have felt when someone else has made fun of you.*

*Do you want to make others feel this way?*

*How do you feel about yourself when you are unkind to someone?*

Sometimes one negative comment can stick with me for a long time. Usually, others say unkind things because they feel insecure about themselves.

*Has this happened to you?*

*What did the person say about you?*

*Do you think everyone feels the same way, or was this person wrong?*

Sarah wants to talk about what she learned during the basketball clinic. She started to understand how to handle her feelings of insecurity, and she wants you to learn, too!

> When I compared myself to others, I felt like I had to prove that I was just as good. My dad helped me realize that everyone has different strengths. I don't have to be good at the same things. When I focus on improving my own skills rather than proving myself to others, I feel better and do better!

*Where or when do you feel out of place?*

*Describe a time you embarrassed yourself by trying to show off or prove yourself.*

*What does an attitude of learning and improving look like?*

> My mom helped me make a list of my good qualities and skills. This helped me see how I can use my strengths and improve on my weaknesses.

*What are your best qualities and strongest skills?*

*What do you like most about yourself?*

*Make these lists in to a poster and put them on your wall as a daily reminder of your strengths.*

> True friends will not make fun of you for your skills or interests. I tried to hide my unusual interest in my ant colony, but it turned out that my friends thought it was cool, too!

*Who are your true friends?*

*What have you learned from a friend who has different interests?*

## How can you help your child understand insecurity and learn confidence?

**Know the Signs.** Kids typically express a low self-esteem and feelings of insecurity in one of two ways: talking negatively about themselves or covering insecurity with false pride. It's easy to identify low self-esteem in a child who expresses their negative self-talk. It takes more careful tuning in to notice it in a child who expresses self-pride. If your child is picking on others, constantly discussing their own accomplishments, or carries a superior attitude toward others, it's likely that your child is actually feeling insecure.

**Honest Positive Talk.** In an attempt to bolster self-esteem, it can be tempting for parents to shower praise on their children when it is not deserved. Receiving false praise may be demotivating and cause a child to mistrust a parent's honest praise at other times. In addition, children who are constantly praised for small tasks may conclude that they are being constantly evaluated, leading to insecurity with constant worries about measuring up. The best kind of praise is specific, honest, and focused on effort rather than results.

The way you talk about yourself and your own accomplishments and failures will influence how your children see their own successes and failures. Practice your own positive self-talk even during difficult moments. A positive mindset in various areas of life will lead to a positive self-image as well.

**Promoting a Kind Inner Voice.** The way you speak to your children will eventually become their own inner voice. Nagging and negativity on your part will produce the same effect in their inner struggles. Conversely, speaking with respect, hope, and problem-solving will help them speak to themselves kindly. Let your children overhear you say positive things about them to others. Resist the urge to make comical complaints about your children to your partner or friends. Always affirm honest compliments that others give to them, and ensure your children know how much you enjoy spending time with them.

**Confidence Crafting.** Help your child see his or her strengths by creating an encouragement craft. Whether you choose a journal, a poster, a collage, or other artwork, help your child create a tangible, visible reminder of his or her strengths and place it in a prominent place.

**Security in a Family Unit.** It is common for siblings to point out the worst in one another. A negative sibling relationship can influence a person's self-concept into adulthood. Get them on the same team by motivating them to encourage one another. Offer a family challenge to fill a jar with compliments or place a sticker on a poster when you notice siblings being kind and encouraging. Make the reward an experience in family fun that leaves everyone with good memories.

**Serving Others.** Help your child find age-appropriate ways to serve others. Low confidence is often a problem of self-centered thoughts of comparison or dwelling on how others view one's self. Serving others may help turn their thoughts outward and boost their mood. It is important for children to feel that they can make a difference in the world. Help your child find local food pantries, animal shelters, elderly or disabled neighbors, or other ways that your child can find regular volunteer opportunities.

*For additional tips and reference information, visit* **www.MVPKids.com**.

Meet the

featured in
## Sarah Sizes Up the Insecure Ant™

**SARAH COHEN-GOLDSTEIN**

Can you also find these MVP Kids®?

**JULIA ROJAS**      **YONG CHEN**

Also featuring…

**ESTER GOLDSTEIN**
"Mom"

**JACOB GOLDSTEIN**
"Dad"

**DAVID COHEN, JR.**
Brother

**ABIGAIL GOLDSTEIN**
Sister

# Grow up with our MVPkids

**Board Books** | **Paperbacks**

  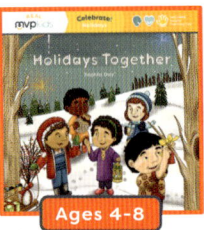
Ages 0-6 | Ages 4-8

Our two **Celebrate!™** series focus on social and emotional needs. Helpful Teaching Tips are included in each book to equip parents, teachers, and counselors. Also available are expertly written curriculum and interactive story apps.

  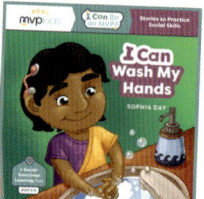

The **I Can Be an MVP™** paperback series helps children ages 2-8 practice social-emotional skills and self-help routines. These short stories are designed with simple, memorable scripts and illustrations focusing on a singular behavior or process.

Our **Mighty Tokens™** paperback series helps emerging readers learn positive concepts with an experienced reader. Each book deposits tokens of affirmation into children so that they may someday become mighty adults.

The **Playful Apprentice™** series is an imaginative view into children's role-playing. These picture books show a variety of community roles and career options that fuel dreams and support character building. Readers will be inspired by interviews and advice from real professionals!

Our **Help Me Become™** series for early elementary readers tells three short stories in each book of our MVP Kids® inspiring character growth. Each story concludes with a discussion guide to help your child process the story and apply the concepts.

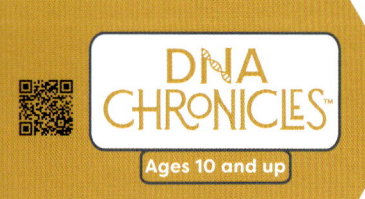 

Step back in time with **DNA Chronicles™**, our historical fiction adventure series. Our MVP Kids® weave together the past and the present, reliving actual historical events to experience the history and culture of their ancestors. In these chapter books, readers will learn about the desire and fortitude it takes to commit to life's most important values, life skills, and accomplishments.

**Help your children grow in character by collecting the entire Help Me Understand™ series!**

Our **Help Me Understand™** series for elementary readers shares the stories of our MVP Kids® learning to understand and manage a specific emotion. Readers will gain tools to take responsibility for their own emotions and develop healthy relationships.

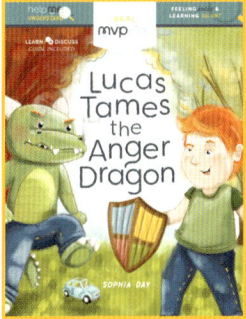 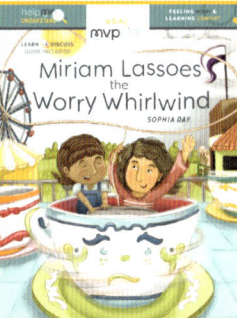 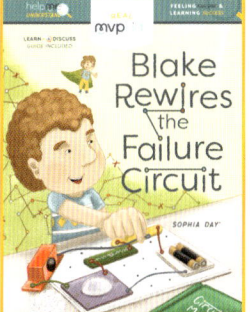 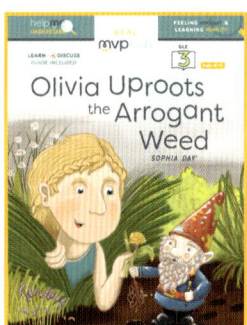

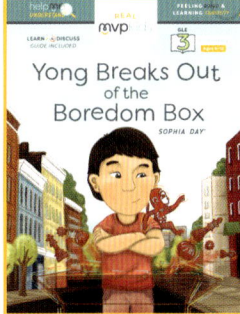 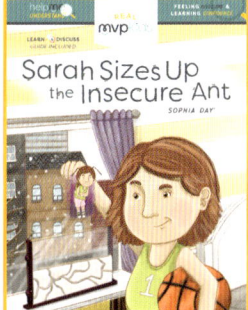 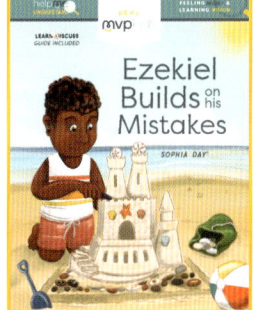 

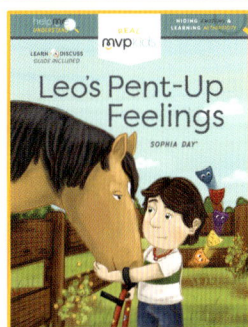 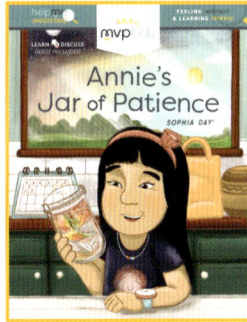 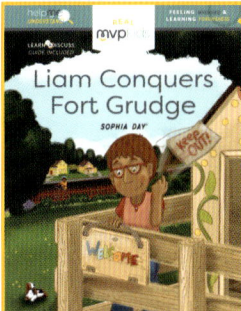 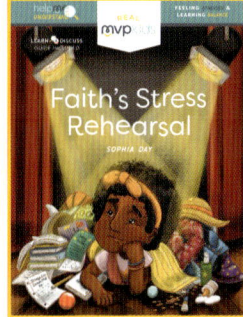

Inspire character with our growing line of products, including books, puppets, SEL programs, music, apps, and more!
**Visit www.MVPKids.com for more information.**

www.MVPKids.com

 Real MVP Kids   @realMVPkids

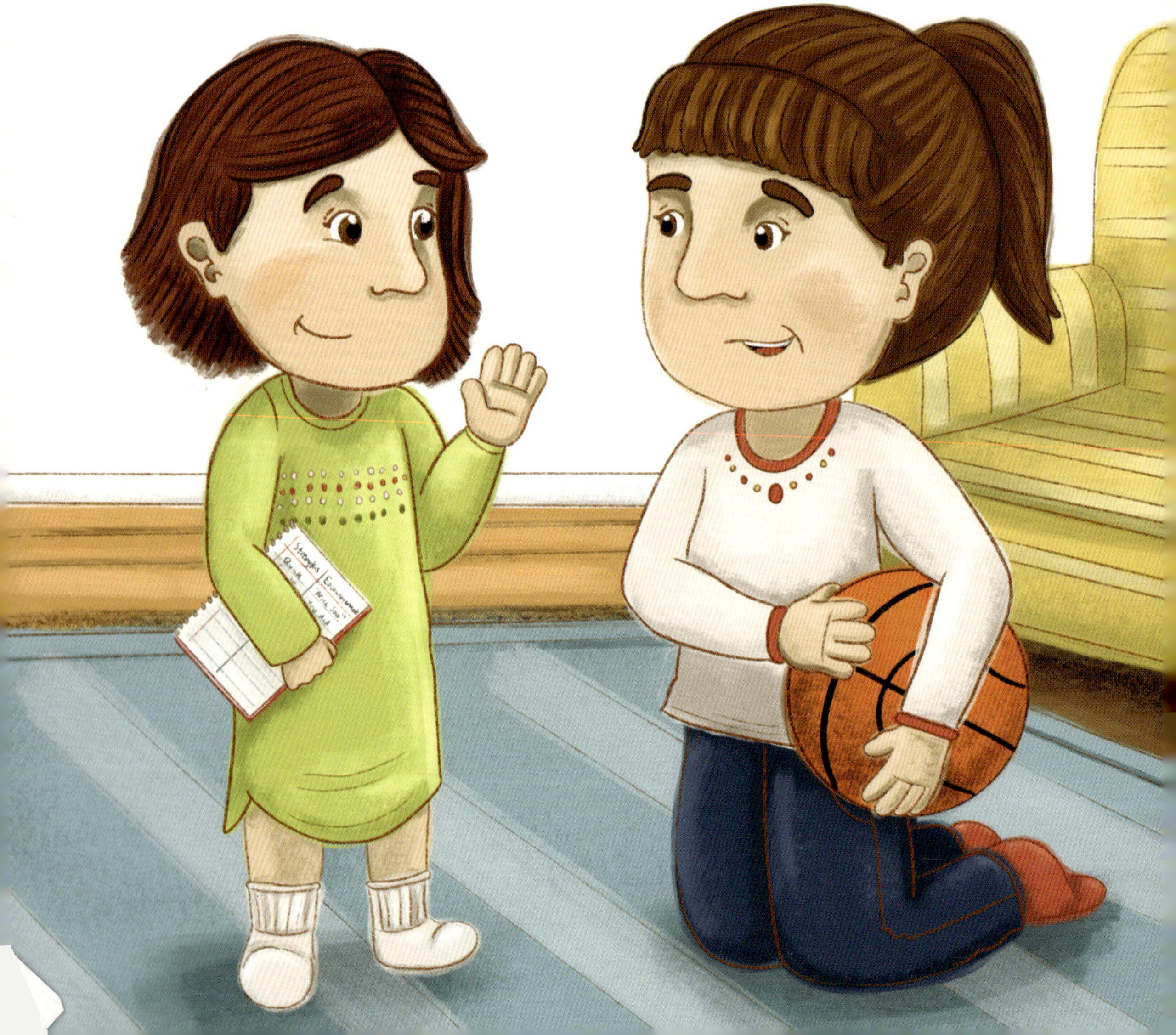